Baby Heart

Remembering Who I Am

KIM KOLZE

ISBN 978-1-63874-739-0 (paperback)
ISBN 978-1-63874-741-3 (hardcover)
ISBN 978-1-63874-740-6 (digital)

Christian Faith Publishing, Inc.
832 Park Avenue
Meadville, PA 16335
www.christianfaithpublishing.com

Printed in the United States of America

To my two lovely children, Emily and Ethan; to God who is inspiring me to follow my dreams.

Meet Baby Heart

She is a beautiful spirit and is filled with inner joy and peace. She knows who she is. She knows where she is from. She knows how to love. She knows her perfection.

She is open-hearted, fearless, and eager to embrace her experience of life. She realizes she will be learning lessons. She realizes some may feel hard. She understands that the lessons are always for her own soul growth to teach her about love and compassion for herself and for others. She also knows that she will forget this and thus spend her lifetime learning to remember.

So the adventure begins.

One day, when Baby Heart was at a park, she was sliding down a slide, laughing loudly. An older woman told her to quiet down and stop screaming.

She said she was sorry. She stopped sliding. She slowly walked home.

She felt sad and decided she was too loud.

(This thought caused a small piece of her red heart to turn black, even though deep inside, there was a still small voice, "You are greatly loved, and perfect as you are.")

Then another day,
Baby Heart's grandfather
gave her a big blue balloon. She
was running while twirling around, and it
accidentally came off her wrist, and her grandfather shook his finger at
her and said that she was bad to have let the balloon go.

She said she was sorry. She stopped running and twirling. She slowly
walked home.

She felt sad and decided she was bad.
(This thought caused a small piece of
her red heart to turn black, even though
deep inside, there
was a still small voice,
"You are greatly loved,
and perfect as you are.")

I'm Sorry.

I am bad

3

One other time, Baby Heart was trying to catch a butterfly and accidentally ran into the back of an older woman. The woman scolded her, saying she needed to pay more attention and to look where she was going.

She said that she was sorry. She stopped chasing the butterflies. She slowly walked home.

She felt sad. She decided she did not pay attention. (This thought caused a small piece of her red heart to turn black, even though deep inside, there was a still small voice, "You are greatly loved, and perfect as you are.")

One day, Baby Heart was at a fountain and saw a shiny penny just below the water. She thought it was beautiful, and she reached in to pick it up to look at it.

A voice came from the other side of the fountain, saying it is not okay to steal.

She said that she was sorry. She dropped the penny back into the fountain. She slowly walked home.

She felt sad and decided she was not very honest.

(This thought caused a small piece of her red heart to turn black, even though deep inside, there was a still small voice, "You are greatly loved, and perfect as you are.")

In school one day, Baby Heart was by herself on a swing, trying to make the swing start to move. As she kicked her legs up in the air, she slipped out of the seat and fell to the ground. A teacher teased her and said she needed to be more careful and maybe swinging was too hard for her.

She said she was sorry. She walked away from the swing set to go sit on a bench. She waited for the end of recess.

She felt sad and decided swinging was too hard for her.

(This thought caused a small piece of her red heart to turn black, even though deep inside, there was a still small voice, "You are greatly loved, and perfect as you are.")

One day, Baby Heart was in gym class, and they were playing dodgeball. She was looking off to the side when a ball hit her on the side of the face and knocked her down. A bully classmate called her dumb and said that next time she should be on the other team.

She said she was sorry. She slowly went to the side of the gym to sit down.

She felt sad and decided she was not good at games.

(This thought caused a small piece of her red heart to turn black, even though deep inside, there was a still small voice, "You are greatly loved, and perfect as you are.")

Then another day, she was to recite a short poem in class. She was nervous and forgot the words. Some of her classmates laughed at her. She felt embarrassed.

She said she was sorry. She slowly walked to her desk.

She felt sad and decided she decided she was stupid.

(This thought caused a small piece of her red heart to turn black, even though deep inside, there was a still small voice, "You are greatly loved, and perfect as you are.")

One day, Baby Heart was with her mom and her dad at the kitchen table at dinner. She was smiling and being silly while reaching for a roll and accidentally knocked her father's cell phone off the kitchen table into the dog's water bowl. Her mom and her dad raised their voices angrily. They said, "Look what you have done now! What is wrong with you? How can you be so clumsy!"

She said she was sorry. She looked down. She started to cry.

She felt sad and decided she was clumsy.

(This thought caused a small piece of her red heart to turn black, even though deep inside, there was a still small voice, "You are greatly loved, and perfect as you are.")

9

The very next day, Baby Heart was feeling discouraged, and she found a bench far away from everyone and sat by herself, tears running down her face. She felt sad. She felt lost. She had lost her sense of who she was. She prayed that somehow she could find her way back to truth, to joy, to happiness.

A moment later, something changed. She felt the warmth of the sun on her face and a slight breeze. Then she wiped her eyes and saw a bluebird on a branch close by. She heard some laughter from afar, and she heard sounds of a creek nearby. She sat up and took a couple of deep breaths and then heard steps behind her.

A beautiful, loving red heart came and sat beside her. He said, "Hi, I am Immanuel Heart. Who are you?" Baby Heart said, "I have forgotten who I am." He said, "Is that so? I know who you are." He put his arm around her and gently said, "You are Baby Heart. You are greatly loved, and perfect as you are." She felt like she had heard that somewhere before, but she couldn't remember yet where.

Immanuel asked her, "Baby Heart, why are you so sad?" Baby Heart answered, "People don't like me—I am too loud." Gently laughing, Immanuel Heart responded, "But that is not true. I know you, and you are not too loud." Baby Heart smiled. Then he said, "We don't always know why people say the things they do. They may feel sad inside. The kindest gesture we can offer is forgiveness. And that is a gift, not only for them, but also for you. Remember that, and remember you are greatly loved and perfect as you are."

She realized she couldn't even remember why she thought she was too loud. She went down the slide.

She felt a sense of relief and kindness and a little happiness.

A piece of red heart healed a piece of her black heart.

A few moments passed. Then Immanuel Heart asked, "Would you like a balloon to cheer you up?" Baby Heart answered, "No, I don't like balloons—I am bad." Gently laughing, Immanuel Heart responded, "I happen to know you like balloons." Baby Heart smiled. Then he said, "We don't always know why people say the things they do. They may feel lonely inside. The kindest gesture we can offer is forgiveness, and that is a gift, not only for them, but also for you. Remember that, and remember you are greatly loved and perfect as you are."

She realized she couldn't even remember why she didn't like balloons and why she thought she was bad. She took the balloon.

She felt a sense of enjoyment and a little more happiness.

A piece of red heart healed a piece of her black heart.

A few moments passed. Then Immanuel Heart said, "Oh, look! A beautiful butterfly." Baby Heart answered, "I don't like butterflies—they cause me to lose my attention." Gently laughing, Immanuel Heart responded, "I happen to know you like butterflies. Go ahead and play with it." Baby Heart smiled. Then he said, "We don't always know why people say the things they do. They may feel scared inside. The kindest gesture we can offer is forgiveness, and that is a gift, not only for them but also for you. Remember that, and remember you are greatly loved and perfect as you are."

She realized she couldn't remember why she didn't like butterflies or why she thought she didn't pay attention. She got up and played with the butterfly.

She felt a sense of wonder and a little more happiness.

A piece of red heart healed a piece of her black heart.

A few moments passed. Then Immanuel Heart said, "Look over there. Would you like to make a wish in the fountain?" Baby Heart answered, "No, I don't go near fountains. I'm not honest." Gently laughing, Immanuel Heart responded, "I happen to know you like fountains, and you are honest. Here is a penny, go make a wish." Baby Heart smiled. Then he said, "We don't always know why people say the things they do. They may feel small inside. The kindest gesture we can offer is forgiveness, and that is a gift, not only for them but also for you. Remember that, and remember you are greatly loved and perfect as you are."

She realized she couldn't remember why she didn't like fountains or why she thought she wasn't honest. She took the penny and made a wish.

She felt a sense of hope and a little more happiness.

A piece of red heart healed a piece of her black heart.

A few moments passed. Then Immanuel Heart asked, "Do you want me to push you on the swings over there?" Baby Heart answered, "No, I've never liked swings. It is too hard for me." Gently laughing, Immanuel Heart responded, "I happen to know you like swinging and you are good at it." Baby Heart smiled. Then he said, "We don't always know why people say the things they do. They may feel anxious inside. The kindest gesture we can offer is forgiveness, and that is a gift, not only for them but also for you. Remember that, and remember you are greatly loved and perfect as you are."

She realized she couldn't remember why she didn't like to swing or why she thought she wasn't good at swinging. She decided to swing.

She felt a sense of playfulness and a little more happiness.

A piece of red heart healed a piece of her black heart.

A few moments passed. Then Immanuel Heart asked, "See those children over there playing dodgeball? Did you play games like that when you were young?" Baby Heart answered, "I wasn't good at dodgeball. I am dumb." Gently laughing, Immanuel Heart responded, "I happen to know you are just fine at dodgeball, and you are not dumb." Baby Heart smiled. Then he said, "We don't always know why people say the things they do. They may feel insecure inside. The kindest gesture we can offer is forgiveness, and that is a gift, not only for them but also for you. Remember that, and remember you are greatly loved and perfect as you are."

She realized she couldn't remember why she didn't like dodgeball or why she thought she was dumb. She played a little dodgeball.

She felt a sense of inner acceptance and a little more happiness.

A piece of red heart healed a piece of her black heart.

A few moments passed. Then Immanuel Heart asked, "How about this: will you share with me one of your favorite poems?" Baby Heart answered, "I can't remember the words to any poems. I am stupid." Gently laughing, Immanuel Heart responded, "I happen to know you have a wonderful memory. Give it a try." Baby Heart smiled. Then he said, "We don't always know why people say the things they do. They may feel lost inside. The kindest gesture we can offer is forgiveness, and that is a gift, not only for them but also for you. Remember that, and remember you are greatly loved and perfect as you are."

She realized she couldn't remember why she thought she was stupid. She recited the exact poem that she had memorized for class.

She felt a sense of confidence and a little more happiness.

A piece of red heart healed a piece of her black heart.

A few moments passed, then Immanuel asked his last question. "You have a wonderful family. Do you realize how much your mother and father love you?" Baby Heart answered, "I often make them mad, I am very clumsy." Gently laughing, Immanuel Heart responded, "I happen to know your mother and father love you very much. They do not see you that way." Baby Heart smiled. Then he said, "We don't always know why people say the things they do, even mommies and daddies. They may feel fearful inside. But we can remember they are greatly loved too. The kindest gesture we can offer is forgiveness. And that is a gift, not only for them but also for you. Remember that, and remember you are greatly loved and perfect as you are."

She realized she couldn't remember why she thought she very clumsy. In fact, she felt very loved..

She felt a sense of worthiness and all of a sudden complete happiness.

(The final piece of red heart heals a piece of her black heart.)

Immanuel gently laughed and said, "Baby Heart— remember this from now on—always listen for the still, small voice inside reminding you that you are greatly loved and perfect as you are. It's often not the loudest voice. It's often not the strongest voice, but it is the true voice."

Baby Heart began to remember what it felt like to be filled with inner joy and peace. She remembered who she was. She remembered where she was from. She remembered how to love. She knew her perfection. She felt herself again.

Baby Heart then realized she had been carrying all these false beliefs about herself for quite some time. She remembered these were the lessons she came to learn, the lessons to teach her about how to have love and compassion for herself and others.

She smiled, gave Immanuel a big hug, and ventured off, open-hearted, fearless, and eager to embrace her experience of life with a sense of excitement and anticipation of what new lessons may come, confident that she would remember. She would always remember.

About the Author

Kim Kolze is a new author who is excited to publish her first book, *Baby Heart—Remembering Who I Am*, which is a children's book with a universal message around love, compassion, forgiveness, and healing.

Kim hopes this story prompts discussion around the idea of false beliefs and how they can alter our innate sense of who we are as beautiful divine beings.

CPSIA information can be obtained
at www.ICGtesting.com
Printed in the USA
JSHW011302110222
22768JS00004B/51